Izabella

12-20-13

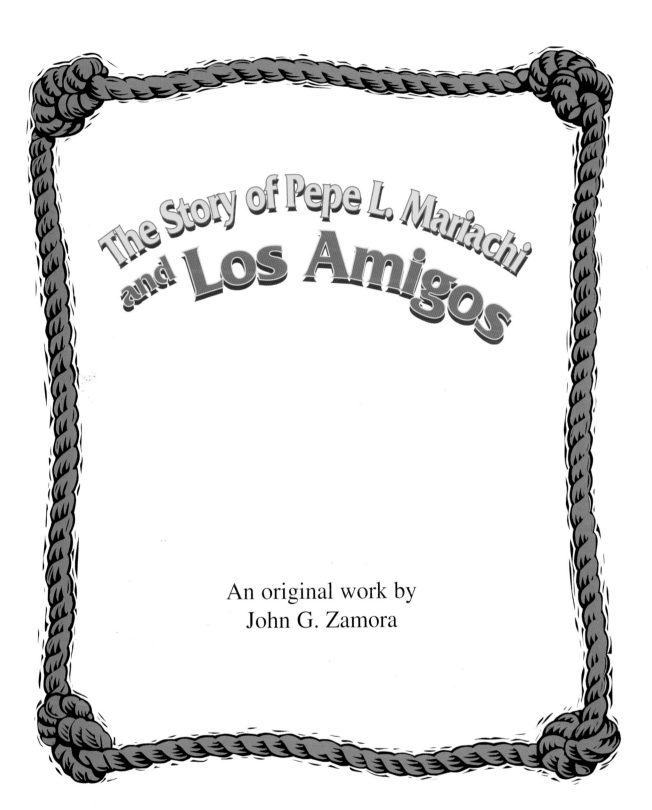

The Story of Pepe L. Mariachi and Los Amigos

An original work by
John G. Zamora

The story of Pepe L. Mariachi and Los Amigos
is an original work by John G. Zamora

Text and Illustrations
©2002 Capitol Development Group
Capitol Developement Group P.O. Box 3000A, San Jose, CA 95156-0001

First Edition

ISBN 0-9720712-0-2

Printed in Hong Kong by South China Printing Company Ltd.

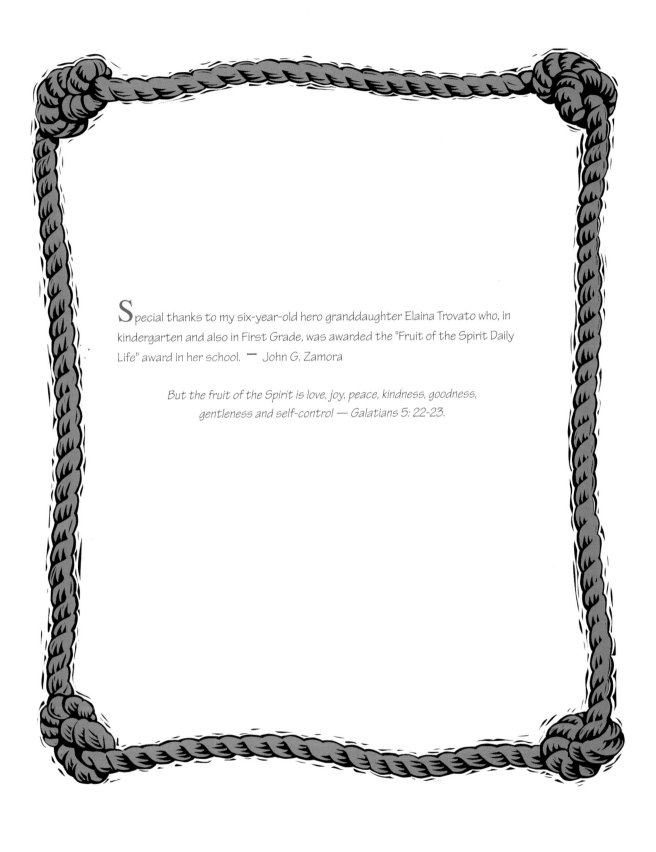

Special thanks to my six-year-old hero granddaughter Elaina Trovato who, in kindergarten and also in First Grade, was awarded the "Fruit of the Spirit Daily Life" award in her school. — John G. Zamora

But the fruit of the Spirit is love, joy, peace, kindness, goodness, gentleness and self-control — Galatians 5: 22-23.

Once upon a time in a small village just north of the Mexican border, there lived a very happy family in a very large hacienda. In the hacienda lived Don Pedro el Patron (the boss) and his beloved wife Doña Maria la Patrona. They had a daughter named Rosita, but everyone called her la Patronicita (the little boss).

Many families worked at the hacienda for Don Pedro, and they all lived happily together in cottages on Don Pedro's land.

The Mariachis were one such lucky family. Juan, a handsome rooster, was strong and intelligent. He taught all of the children of the village reading, writing and music.

His lovely wife Lola, cooked for Don Pedro and Doña Maria.

Their two children, daughter Tita and her older brother Pepe, were excellent musicians, and they loved to sing. Pepe was especially entertaining, and he proudly called himself "Pepe L. Mariachi!" whenever people asked his name.

A family of donkeys also lived on the hacienda… Beto el Burro, his wife Lupe, and their son Paco, whom they called Paquito. The Burros were in charge of farming the hacienda land. They plowed the fields, planted the seeds, and harvested the crops.

Paco was a very good horseman and loved to dress like a vaquero (cowboy) as his father did.

3

The hacienda watchdogs were the Jose Perro family — father Jose, his wife Sofia, and their son Panchito.

The three of them cared for the hacienda's cows, horses, and sheep, and they warned Don Pedro of any dangers that might threaten the hacienda and the families that lived there.

Panchito, loved history, and he would often talk about some of his heroes, men such as Abraham Lincoln, Cesar Chavez, and Martin Luther King, Jr. When he grew up, he hoped to be brave like them and accomplish great things.

One bright and sunny day, watchdog Jose saw in the distance a group of bandidos (bandits) who were coming to the hacienda to steal the animals and other valuables. Quickly, he ran to warn everyone.

"Don Pedro, Don Pedro," he cried. "The bandidos are coming and we must prepare to defend the hacienda."

"You've done good work, Jose" said Don Pedro. "Hurry. Help me get all the children to our under ground hiding place so they will be safe. There are comfortable beds and plenty of food in there, so they will be well cared for until the trouble passes."

With that, Jose, Juan, Beto el Burro, and all the other fathers ushered their precious children into the hiding place and bid them goodbye. "Children, be brave and remember we love you. Stay in hiding for at least five days unless we come for you sooner."

With the sound of galloping horses nearing the hacienda, the men left to protect their land and possessions from the invaders. Even from a distance, the villagers could see that the bandidos were mean. Their rough, unshaven faces were scary and unfeeling.

When the bandidos finally arrived, the men and women of the hacienda were ready to defend what they had worked so hard for. Armed with their wits and bravery, they engaged in a fierce battle. Clouds of dust hid the hacienda from view, and thunderous noises filled the air.

The dust began to settle, and many horses galloped away rider-less, but the bandidos, sadly, had won. The grounds were littered with fallen hacienda defenders, some badly injured. Many others were chased off the grounds or fled to safety. Meanwhile, the bandidos carried off furniture, jewelry, food, and animals, and they set fire to all the buildings.

From their hiding place, the children could hear that the battle had subsided, and they began to question where their parents were. Frightened and alone, they wondered aloud what they should do.

"My father told us to wait until the grown-ups came for us," said Pepe L. Mariachi, "but I'm starting to get worried. The fighting has been over for a long while, and no one has come for us."

"Maybe they need our help," said Tita. "I want to *go see*."

"OK, I think it's safe for us to sneak out of here. Follow me, and be very quiet," said Pepe.

Slowly, Pepe, his sister Tita, Paquito el Burrito, Panchito el Perrito, Senorita Rosita and the rest of the children climbed out of their hiding place. When they emerged, they were devastated by what the bandidos had done to their home.

10

Their beautiful hacienda had been burned to the ground, and all the neighboring houses were ransacked, emptied of their furniture and clothing. All horses and cows had been stolen or fled in fear, and only a few chickens remained, scratching at the dry ground looking for food.

But worst of all, none of the children's parents were there.

"Papa, mama," cried Rosita. "Where are you?" Pepe, in a voice softened by sorrow, said, "I don't know where any of our parents are, but we must go look for them. Follow me and don't worry. If we stick together, we'll make it."

Joining hands, the children started away from the hacienda, hoping one day to return with their families. Pausing for a moment, they turned to take one last look at their beloved home, staring in disbelief of all that had happened just a short time ago.

J ust then, one of the villagers who had worked for Don Pedro approached them. Exhausted from the battle, he told the children, "Your parents are no longer with us. I'm sorry."

The children's eyes followed his as he looked up towards the sky. Bright golden rays of light were shining out from a large white cloud. They knew then that they were orphans.

"I must go look for my own family now," said the man. "Be secure in knowing that your parents will be looking after you."

Pepe and his amigos (friends) continued their journey away from the hacienda to build a new life together. They earned money for food and lodging by singing songs and playing music that Juan Mariachi had taught them in school.

One day while eating together under a shady tree, the children saw a great beam of light shining down from the sky, and it was coming toward them! As the light neared, it got brighter and brighter, and it finally came to rest directly above them. Then, they heard a voice from the heavens.

"Pepe, Pepe L. Mariachi," said the voice, "Your parents are safe with me now." As the voice spoke, the children stared in wonder as they saw the faces of their parents in the sky, coming into clear focus. To their amazement, the faces were smiling.

The voice continued, "You have been called upon for a special mission. From this day forward, you will each have special powers beyond your wildest imagination. Because you have suffered so greatly, and because you are honest and good of heart, you have been chosen to help those who are victimized by bullies, criminals, and those who suffer injustice. You must help young people reject drugs, gangs, and crime. You shall become famous, but you must use your power and fame to help others."

"Your special powers will remain hidden until someone is in need. When it is time to use your powers, you must join hands, forming a circle of love and respect. Then one of you must say the words, 'Los Amigos!'"

The voice finished speaking, and the happy faces of their parents began to fade from the sky. Before they were gone, the parents said, "Remember, we love you and will always be here if you need us. All you have to do is call us. You have the power now."

A few days later, as the friends were enjoying a day in the park, Pepe found himself wondering if the voice and visions had all been a dream. The Amigos, as they were now called, had not yet used their new powers.

Just then the friends saw a boy getting pushed around by a group of bullies who wanted to steal the boy's money. They were very mean, laughing at the frightened boy and knocking to the ground an old man who had rushed to help him.

The brutality was too much for Pepe to watch. Remembering the voice, he decided this would be a good time to see if he and his friends really did have special powers. So, The Amigos gathered in a circle and held hands, and Pepe called out "Los Amigos!" just as he had been told to do.

The echo of his cry was still in the air when a bright flash of light and a cloud of smoke obscured The Amigos from view for several seconds. When the light subsided, The Amigos were dressed in brightly colored Charro (Mexican Cowboy)-style outfits, each identical except for the colors. Attached to their belts were all manner of gadgets and tools, and on their wrists were tiny radios they could use to talk to each other.

Stunned by their new uniforms, they almost forgot to help the boy and man, who were still being harassed by the ruffians. Suddenly, they heard the voices of their parents from above saying, "Don't be afraid now—you have the power!

Pepe turned to his friends and cried, "Amigos Arriba!" and with that, the five rushed to help the boy and old man.

Pepe grabbed the gang leader and pinned his hands behind his back. Before the other gangsters could attack Pepe, the rest of The Amigos came to his aid. Using their new-found abilities, they subdued the gangsters with their speed, strength, and quick thinking. The gangsters soon fled, knowing they could not win.

The little boy, Juanito, and the old man, his grandfather Señor Garcia, were relieved to be safe. Señor Garcia told Pepe that Juanito was the only family he had, since the boy's parents had been killed in an airplane accident. He was therefore especially grateful that Juanito had not been hurt, and to show his appreciation, he invited The Amigos to his home.

"Would you please join us for dinner? I can see that Juanito wants to spend some more time with you, and I would like to as well."

When The Amigos failed to answer right away, Señor Garcia said, "I would like to ask your parents for permission so I can tell them about the good deed you have done today."

Pepe then explained to Señor Garcia that they were all orphans. When Juanito heard this, he was comforted. All of his other friends had parents, and it was sad to hear them talk about the fun they had with their families. But The Amigos, like him, had no parents. When Señor Garcia heard this, he insisted The Amigos come to dinner, and The Amigos agreed.

On their way to dinner, a brilliant ray of light shot through the clouds and shone down on them—just like before, when they learned about their special powers. Again, the same voice said, "Amigos, in order to be transformed back to your normal selves, you must once again form a circle, hold hands, and say Los Amigos!"

So, following these orders, the Amigos formed a circle, and Pepe cried out "Los Amigos!" Flashes of light obscured the Amigos from view, and when it subsided, the Amigos were once again dressed in their normal clothes.

Señor Garcia's house was a big and beautiful mansion. When The Amigos saw it, many of them wanted to leave, feeling out of place in such surroundings. But Señorita Rosita insisted that they stay.

"Please, Pepe," she said. "It's been such a long time since we've had a nice meal, and in a real dining room. I think we *deserve* it, and I, for one, don't feel out of place," she exclaimed, referring to her former role as patroncita of her family's hacienda.

When she said this, the other Amigos began to laugh, for Rosita's face was dirty and her clothing was tattered. She hardly looked like the privileged girl she used to be. But she was still beautiful and carried herself with an air of importance. "I'm going in. You can join me or stay outside," she said

So, The Amigos approached the front door and rang the bell. A butler answered the door. "May I help you?" he asked, a bit perplexed by the appearance of the five youngsters standing before him. Señor Garcia rarely had guests, but when he did, they usually looked very different from this group.

Señorita Rosita, confident as usual, said, "We have been invited to dinner by Señor... Señor...," but she had forgotten the old man's name. As she looked around for help, Pepe said, "Garcia. Señor Garcia."

By this time, Señor Garcia had heard voices and hurried to the door to greet his guests.

He almost didn't recognize The Amigos, as they were no longer wearing their colorful uniforms. "What happened?" He asked. "You look so different. Well," he added, deciding not to press the issue, "I am happy to see you. Please come in. Dinner is almost ready."

Following Señor Garcia to the dining room, The Amigos were impressed with the elegance and beauty of his mansion. Everything they saw—the furniture, paintings, and other decor—was gorgeous.

The Amigos were served the best dinner they had eaten since leaving their village. They ate heartily, their appetites satisfied by numerous tasty dishes.

After dinner, Juanito invited The Amigos to play soccer with him in the backyard, and what fun they had kicking the ball, running, and laughing! After each team had scored a few points, Paquito accidentally kicked the ball over a row of hedges. When Panchito and Tita went to fetch it, they found a marvelous surprise.

There before them was a deserted hacienda, its paint faded and windows boarded shut. It was surrounded by a barren field and dilapidated corrals. Though it was run down, it reminded them of the hacienda where they used to live.

Tita called out to her brother. "Pepe, Pepe, come see what we found!"

Pepe hurried to her with the rest of The Amigos and Juanito close behind. Staring at the old hacienda, he asked, "Doesn't it remind you of our home? It brings back so many memories of our parents." They all stood silent, tears running down their cheeks, reflecting back on how their lives used to be.

They were startled out of their thoughts by Señor Garcia. "Juanito! Muchachos! Where are you?" he cried. "Is everything OK?"

"Yes, grandfather, we're just playing," replied Juanito. With that, they all went back to the yard to finish their game.

As it began to get dark outside, Pepe announced it was time for The Amigos to leave. "We have a busy day tomorrow," he said. "Thank you for having us over."

"Where will you stay tonight?" asked Señor Garcia. "Why don't you stay here with us? I can take care of you, and you can be family for Juanito. He has come to love you so."

"Thank you very much. Señor Garcia," said Pepe, "but we cannot accept your offer. We would love to stay with you and Juanito, but, you see, we have a mission and must be free to come and go at a moment's notice, whenever we are needed."

Confused by what Pepe said, Señor Garcia asked them what kind of mission five young orphans could be involved in. When they didn't answer, he said, "Maybe I can help you."

Thinking this over, Pepe realized how hard it would be on his friends growing up homeless, constantly moving around and sleeping in a different place every night. Finally, he spoke. "Señor Garcia, I have an idea. Tell me why the hacienda behind your mansion is abandoned."

"I am old," Señor Garcia replied, "and I lost interest in the land when my only son, Juanito's father, passed away."
"What if we restore the hacienda and work the land for you?" asked Pepe. "In exchange, you could let us live there. It reminds us so much of our home, and I promise that we would take very good care of it."

Señor Garcia replied, "That would be splendid! Tomorrow I will get all of the carpenters and painters we'll need." "That won't be necessary Señor Garcia," said Pepe. "We must earn our keep and do our own work. All our own work."

The old man smiled and shook Pepe's hand. "It's a deal," he said. "I am very happy you will be living with us, and Juanito will be thrilled!"

When all was settled, everyone hugged each other, filled with joy and excitement. The Amigos gathered together and held hands. Pepe said, "I'm proud of all of you. We stuck together, and now we're a family again."

"But don't forget," said Señorita Rosita, "that I will be the Patrona."

"Yes, Rosita," they all said. Of course they all knew that Pepe would be the Patron.

In the days that followed, The Amigos busied themselves repairing the corral, preparing the soil for planting, and restoring the hacienda to its original beauty. By the end of the week, the corral was fixed, the land was planted with seeds, and the house looked like new.

Pepe, Paco, and Panchito were resting on the front porch, admiring their work, when Señor Garcia drove up with Juanito. They brought a dining table for the Amigo's new home.

The timing could not have been more perfect! Tita and Señorita Rosita had just finished preparing a wonderful feast to celebrate. That night, The Amigos and their new family ate, laughed, and sang songs, rejoicing in their happy home, full of love just like the old days.

The next day was the first day of school for Juanito and The Amigos. They were all ready to go except Señorita Rosita, who always took a little extra time to groom herself.

"It's time to go," Pepe called out to her. "We don't want to be late on our first day."

Juanito and the rest of The Amigos began walking, and soon Rosita caught up to them. They looked like any typical group of youngsters, happily on their way to school. It was a lovely spring day. The sun was out, flowers were blooming, and the birds were filling the air with their song.

Señor Garcia, watching them from a window in his bedroom, began to think about his mysterious new friends. What did they mean by "their mission," he wondered. And why were they so eager to help him and Juanito, who were strangers to them?

"Well, all I know is that they are beautiful children, and I have come to love them, as Juanito has," he said to himself. "He is so happy now, and so am I."

The Amigos had a good first day at school, registering for classes and meeting new friends. On their way home, as they were walking by a farmhouse, they saw three men stealing some sheep. Looking through the front windows of the house, they could see that the farmer and his wife were both tied to their chairs, unable to move. The Amigos looked at each other, and they all knew what they had to do.

Pepe turned to Juanito and said, "Run home and tell your grandfather to call the police. We'll join you a little later. Just keep running," he said, "and don't look back."

As Juanito started home, The Amigos went behind some bushes, held hands, and yelled out "Los Amigos!" As before, flashes of light and a cloud of smoke obscured them from view. Seconds later, it cleared, revealing the brave group of five in their bright uniforms.

And so began The Amigos second chance to fulfill their mission...

This ends this episode of Pepe L. Mariachi and Los Amigos, but only the beginning of their adventures as they fight for justice against crime and evil.

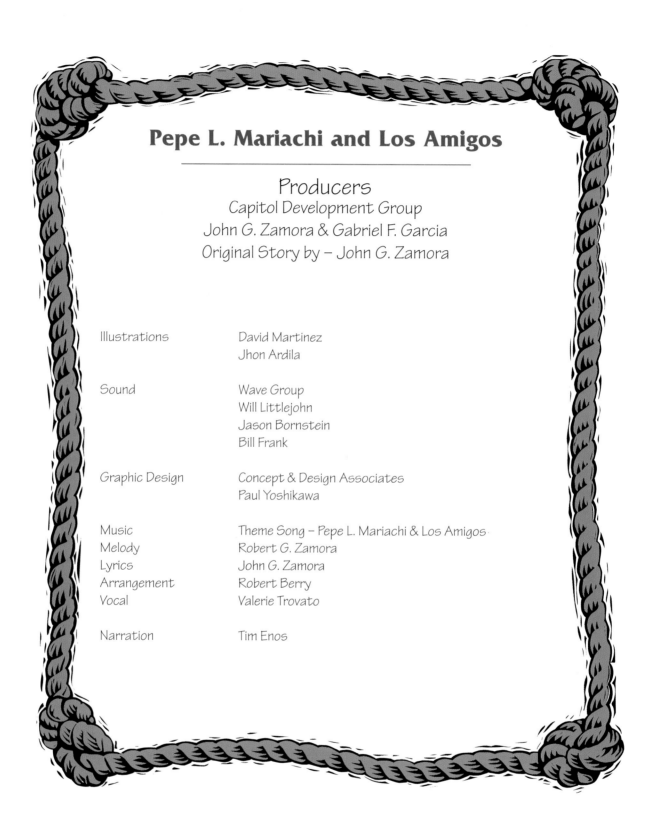

Pepe L. Mariachi and Los Amigos

Producers
Capitol Development Group
John G. Zamora & Gabriel F. Garcia
Original Story by – John G. Zamora

Illustrations	David Martinez
	Jhon Ardila
Sound	Wave Group
	Will Littlejohn
	Jason Bornstein
	Bill Frank
Graphic Design	Concept & Design Associates
	Paul Yoshikawa
Music	Theme Song – Pepe L. Mariachi & Los Amigos
Melody	Robert G. Zamora
Lyrics	John G. Zamora
Arrangement	Robert Berry
Vocal	Valerie Trovato
Narration	Tim Enos